I AM READING

Doctor Witch's Animal Hospital

SHEILA MAY BIRD

ILLUSTRATED BY

EMMA PARRISH

KINGFISHER
NEW YORK

To Mum, who still likes to hear my stories—S. M. B.
For my mum, with oodles of love—E. P.

JBC / Am Reading

KINGFISHER
LONDON & NEW YORK

Text copyright © 2007 by Sheila May Bird
Illustrations copyright © 2007 by Emma Parrish
Published in the United States by Kingfisher,
175 Fifth Ave., New York, NY 10010
Kingfisher is an imprint of Macmillan Children's Books, London.
All rights reserved.

Distributed in the U.S. by Macmillan, 175 Fifth Ave., New York, NY 10010
Distributed in Canada by H.B. Fenn and Company Ltd., 34 Nixon Road,
Bolton, Ontario L7E 1W2

LIBRARY OF CONGRESS CATALOGING-IN-PUBLICATION DATA
Bird, Sheila.
Doctor Witch's animal hospital / Sheila May Bird; illustrated by Emma Parrish.
p. cm. -- (I am reading)
Summary: A witch who treats animals heals some sick patients on her way to the wizards' ball.
ISBN 978-0-7534-5977-5
[1. Witches--Fiction. 2. Animals--Fiction. 3. Magic--Fiction.] I. Parrish, Emma, ill. II. Title.
PZ7.B51196Do 2007
[Fic]--dc22
2007023849

ISBN: 978-0-7534-5977-5

BT/AZ 6/12 $3.99

Kingfisher books are available for special promotions and premiums. For details contact:
Special Markets Department, Macmillan, 175 Fifth Avenue, New York, NY 10010.

For more information, please visit www.kingfisherpublications.com

Printed in China
2 4 6 8 10 9 7 5 3

Contents

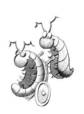

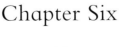

Chapter One

Doctor Imelda Witch lived in a pretty cottage. It had a curved roof and a crooked chimney.

Around the cottage was a garden where
Doctor Witch grew the plants for her
spells and potions, ointments, and lotions.
It was a pretty garden, but a smelly
one too.

Doctor Witch's
Animal Hospital

Doctor Witch arrived back at her cottage after a very busy morning. She had been helping a beetle give birth to 130 baby beetles.

Doctor Witch was a vet—a special doctor who cares for animals.

Now her cottage was full of animals, all waiting to see her.

"First, please," she called.

"That's me," said a very tiny voice.

Clomp, clomp, ouch, clomp, clomp . . .

"Ah, Mr. Centipede," said Doctor Witch, looking down. "How can I help you?"

"I've hurt my leg," replied the centipede. He painfully waved one of his many legs at her.

With a twitch of her nose and a flick of
her wand . . .

. . . Doctor Witch shrank herself to the
size of the centipede.

"Oh, dear," said Doctor Witch. "I'm afraid that your leg is broken. But with my spells and potions, ointments, and lotions, I'm sure that I can help."

She mixed up a potion and bandaged the broken leg.

"It's just as well that you've got 99 other legs to use," she said.

The grateful centipede left.

Clomp, clomp, clomp, clomp, thud, clomp, clomp . . .

"Next, please," called Doctor Witch.

Chapter Two

That day Doctor Witch used her spells and potions, ointments, and lotions to help:

a badger with bad breath . . .

. . . a deer with dizziness . . .

. . . a fox with the flu . . .

. . . a weasel with a
wobbly tooth . . .

. . . a rabbit with
a rash . . .

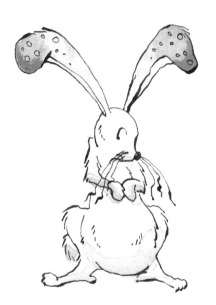

. . . and a squirrel
with a squint.

She closed the door as her last patient left.

An owl flew into it.

"Ouch!" said the owl. "I think I've broken my beak."

"I'm very sorry," said Doctor Witch.

She looked at the owl's beak. It looked sore, but it was not broken.

The owl gave Doctor
Witch an invitation.
"For me?" said Doctor
Witch. "How exciting!"

You are invited to the annual wizard and witch ball. It is this Saturday at the Grand Hall. Please reply using the delivery owl.

Doctor Witch
was delighted.

She wrote a reply. "Yes,
please! I would love to
come. Thank you!"

17

Chapter Three

Doctor Witch was very excited.

The important question was, what would she wear?

She could wear her long, straight, jet-black dress.

She could wear
her long, flowing,
night-black dress.

But she definitely
wouldn't wear her
short, frilly, coal-black
dress, because it showed
her knobby knees!

19

Which hat should she wear? Bendy points were popular, but she had always preferred a tall, slender point.

She went to bed dreaming of handsome
wizards and chocolate cake.

The next morning, Doctor Witch mixed together some wildflowers in her cauldron.

She mixed Toad's Foot and Hare's Bell . . .

. . . with some Old Man's Beard . . .

. . . and added some Bird's
Foot for good measure.

Then she put the potion into
a bottle, ready for her bath
on Saturday.

Saturday came quickly. Doctor Witch enjoyed getting ready for the ball.

She took the frogs and newts out of the bathtub before she got in.

She poured the potion into the hot water, making rainbow-colored bubbles.

She polished her black nails . . .

. . . her black boots . . .

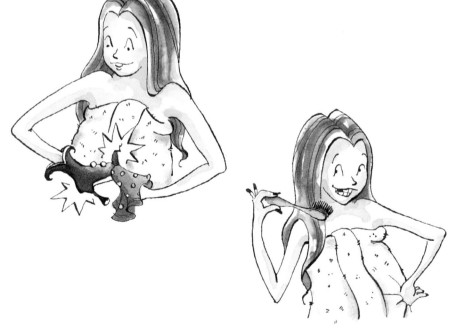

. . . and even her black tooth.

Once she was dressed, she looked into her magic mirror.

"Mirror, mirror, on the wall, how do I look?"

"Not bad at all!" it replied.

She gave herself a satisfied smile and
got her broomstick from the shed.
Then she packed a selection of spells and
potions, ointments, and lotions into her
portable first-aid kit.

In no time at all, she was off to the ball.

Chapter Four

She hadn't flown far when she heard a
worried hiss from the grass below.
"Pleasssse come to *sssse*e my baby.
He ha*ssss* bitten hi*ssss* own tongue."
With a twitch of her nose and a flick of
her wand, Doctor Witch was the size of a
snake. She followed the mother snake
through the grass.

"Don't worry. With my spells and potions, ointments, and lotions, I'll soon have your tongue fixed," she told the baby snake.

And she did.

"You're *sssso* kind," hissed the snakes.

With a twitch of her nose and a flick of
her wand, Doctor Witch was back on her
way to the ball. But now her tall, slender
hat was bent. She had grass seeds in her
hair and mud on her face.

"Bother!" she said when she caught sight
of herself in a puddle.

She hadn't gone far when she heard
another noise. In a tall tree, two owls
were flapping in their nest.
"Up here!" they hooted. "Up here!"
Doctor Witch pointed her
broomstick toward the tree.

31

"Our baby has fallen out of the nest!"
cried the owls.

Doctor Imelda Witch could see the
baby owl caught in the lower branches
of the tree.

"I can't do a lot with
my spells and potions,
ointments, and lotions.
But I think I can reach
him with my broomstick,"
she said.

By weaving the broomstick through the
branches, Doctor Witch was able to
rescue the fallen bird. She took him back
to his nest.

"Thank you, thank you," hooted the grateful owls. "You're welcome," she replied.

But now her dress was torn, and she had lost one of her well-polished black boots. "Bother! Bother!" she said.

Chapter Five

Doctor Witch arrived at the ball. She was very late. Her dress was torn, and her pointed hat was bent. One of her shoes was missing. She had grass seeds in her hair. She had mud on her face.

But worst of all, she had lost her wand!

"Oh, very big bother!" she said.

She showed her crumpled invitation to the wizard at the door.

"You can't come in here looking like that," he said. "Go away."

She had been looking forward to meeting handsome wizards. She had been looking forward to eating chocolate cake even more.

Poor Doctor Witch. She had only been trying to be helpful.

Without her wand, she couldn't even cast a clean-up spell.

Chapter Six

One of the owls whose baby Doctor
Witch had rescued landed on the wizard's
shoulder. He cooed into the wizard's ear.

"I say," called the wizard to Doctor
Witch, "this owl tells me that you saved
his baby."

"All part of a day's work,"
replied Doctor Witch
modestly.

There was a rustling around the wizard's feet and some muffled hissing.

"Mrs. Snake says that you stopped her baby's tongue from bleeding," remarked the wizard.

"It was the least I could do," said Doctor Witch sincerely.

"Any witch as caring as you have been deserves to go to the ball," said the wizard.

"Excuse me," said a very small voice from the wizard's toe. "I found this. I think it belongs to the vet." The centipede with the bandaged leg had a wand balanced on his back.

"Oh, thank you!" cried Doctor Witch. And with a twitch of her nose and a flick of her wand, she looked neat and clean again.

Doctor Witch had a wonderful time. She danced with handsome wizards until her feet ached and she had to take off her well-polished boots.

But, best of all, Doctor Witch ate a lot of chocolate cake.

About the author and illustrator

Sheila May Bird used to work as a nanny and a nursery school teacher. Nowadays she enjoys writing children's stories. "I wish I could twitch my nose and do magic like Doctor Witch," she says. Sheila lives in Surrey, England.

Emma Parrish has had several children's books published. Emma says, "I was so pleased that Doctor Witch enjoyed the ball in the end. She deserved it after being so kind to the animals." Emma was born and still lives in Wales, in a beautiful old farmhouse with her sheepdog, Leah.

Strategies for Independent Readers

Predict

Think about the cover, illustrations, and the title
of the book. What do you think this book will be about?
While you are reading think about what may
happen next and why.

Monitor

As you read ask yourself if what you're
reading makes sense. If it doesn't, reread, look
at the illustrations, or read ahead.

Question

Ask yourself questions about important ideas
in the story such as what the characters might
do or what you might learn.

Phonics

If there is a word that you do not know, look carefully
at the letters, sounds, and word parts that you do know.
Blend the sounds to read the word. Ask yourself if this is
a word you know. Does it make sense in the sentence?

Summarize

Think about the characters, the setting where the
story takes place, and the problem the characters faced
in the story. Tell the important ideas in the beginning,
middle, and end of the story.

Evaluate

Ask yourself questions like: Did you like the story?
Why or why not? How did the author make the story
come alive? How did the author make the story fun to
read? How well did you understand the story? Maybe
you can understand it better if you read it again!

THE MARK TWAIN LIBRARY
P.O. BOX 1009
REDDING, CT 06875